BEHIND THE SMILE

Collection of Biographical poetry in free verse form

By

Annaliza V. Aquino

Copyright © 2021 BEHIND THE SMILE by Annaliza V. Aquino

Published by Poetry Planet Book Publishing House
Designed and arranged by Tess Ritumalta
Edited by Richmond Rodsteel

Please submit all reviews and comments or report errors to anna9_villegas@yahoo.com.

Photo used courtesy of Pinterest and Pixabay and may contain its own copywrites.

ISBN:
Hardbound- 978-621-8253-93-3
Softbound- 978-621-8253-92-6
Mobile/Kindle- 978-621-8253-94-0

DEDICATION

This book is dedicated to my late grandfather, Florentino S. Villegas and grandmother, Adelina E. Villegas who often pushed me to be their better version. Taught me life's lessons and believed that I could go far beyond my expectations, that dreams can be reached one step at a time...I hope that they are with me now witnessing the realities of my dreams. This book will remind me that life is not an easy journey but everyone has a perfect time in God's own ways.

ACKNOWLEDGEMENTS

Big thanks to those who believe in my talent especially to my family, my backbone.

To my children, Lucille Anthonette and Marc Regienald, my brother, Remegio Jr and sisters, Princess and Maria Luremn for believing in my passion and giving their full support.

To my better half, for making this dream possible.

To mami Zenaida Navarro for opening the door and introducing me to a group of poets and writers, and who also made me believe that writing poems is not only a passion but also a confidence booster. This has been my lifelong dream.

Thank you to Menchu Rama who never gave up on me in all aspects of my journeys in life.

To all the poetry groups I belong for accepting me in their literary world.

Thank you God Almighty for having this wonderful and contented life.

Agyamanak kanyayo amen apo.
Baleg ya salamat ed sikayon amen.
Maraming Salamat po sa inyong lahat.
Thank you very much to all.

PREFACE

Behind that sweet smile, there's a story you would never understand. The pain that kept and sealed in written words, the happiness behind closed doors, some stories remain unsealed and silently carried. How love grew and how it faded. These are   the recollections of all the emotions of the author and expression of how grateful she is in meeting every person inside this book. Unfolding those that happened without regrets.

TABLE OF CONTENTS

This relationship is
going to kill me

MRS UNIVERSE... MY MOTHER EARTH

This poem is not enough, to let you know how
grateful and blessed I am for being your daughter.
But still I made it for you, to remind you that I will
always be here to love you forever.
Those good manners and proper conduct that
you've taught me will be in my mind and in my
heart together.
The love of God above all, that you bestowed on
me will be shared to my friends and loved ones
altogether.

You're an epitome of that greatest love of all,

You always lift me up in times of disappointments
and especially in my worst and drowning soul.
You taught me how to be strong and until now you
help me wipe my tears and still treat me as your
princess girl.
I love you is not enough to say thank you for
bringing me out of this wonderful world.

She is my beloved mother,
LUCITA is her name,
She is God servant,
Faithful wife,
Respected leader,
Helpful friend,
Generous sister and all praises are not enough to
describe her; after all I need to be good at my
compliments so she will give me an extra
allowance when she gets hers.

Dear Mom, don't worry about me,
I have become what you wanted me to be.
Things that they see don't matter anymore,
I know I have fulfilled your dreams on me.
I have a beautiful heart and wonderful intentions
any Mom would love to be.
Thank you for raising me well and for being the
Mrs. Universe in our family.

Someday, I can repay you, not just a poem for you, but a true to life story to share to those who really care.

WOMAN FOR ALL SEASONS

She is my adviser, preacher and soon to be
godmother.
She is a businesswoman and a pet lover.
She is a dedicated friend and a passionate
sister.
She is indeed an epitome of a loving wife and a
great mother.

She loves her friends and shares them her
wisdom,
She can even be a dietician, a plant lover and a
beautician all in one, you can message her any
time, even when she's doing her favorite
pastime. She will attend to you as quick as she
can.

You will never feel alone, she's someone you
can lean on.

She helps her siblings and her neighbors too.
She goes to charity works but she doesn't want
others to know.
She has a good heart that God only see.
I know this because she still helps me even
while I'm overseas.

She is MENCHU, the Woman for All Seasons.
She can teach you how to carry yourself and
how to move on.
She knows a lot about life and learns from her
in all occasions. Indeed, she is a woman with
powerful motivation, and I love her without
pretentions.

ONAD...THE ARTIST

I met him in Horizons page. Home for talented
migrants,
And he is really a gem and a passionate tyrant,
Of his masterpieces that are relevant,
Really extraordinary and he can finish in an instant.

I admire him a lot; he is an artist rare to find,
This is all i can do, for him, being so kind,
Thank you for his artwork we have memories to
bind,
And forever a remembrance in my mind.

One day, we will meet with joy
And eat together with our favorite chicken joy
Don't worry brother, I will not ask you to pay for it
But if you insist I would love to take it.

This poem is for you, my virtual friend,

Take care always and continue to reach the good
end,
For I felt your sincerity and passion,
Love for an art is your awesome dedication.

Kuya Onad Hernandez inspired me for this piece.
Thank you for sharing your awesome talent to us.

THE LADY RIDER

She is JESSABEL not that Dyesebel, but they are
both experts in their chosen field. When she hits the
road, you'd better fasten your seat belt,
For you will travel that place and she will give you
an amazing ride. Oppps, don't worry she is a
wonderful friend, a lady expert driver even the
road has tides.

She is my two in one friend, she can be a gorgeous
teacher and a furious rider in between. She is witty,
lovely, funny but fearless in the end.
She is adventurous and she wants to take you
there,
So you can see beautiful places and also feel the
cool breeze with care.

When this pandemic ends, I will be home to
backride with her,
I will wear my full gears to be safe and experience
flying with her, discover her passion and share
moments with her,
In the end, we will close our journey with joys and
laughter.

MIA MIA dear, I wish you all the best that life can
offer you,
You may not reach the tip but I admire your
courage and strength,
To face trials and tests,
Life is like riding in your two wheel drive, be safe,
stay alert, and focus on your destination and hit
that button with pride.

ESTER THE FIGHTER

She is indeed my virtual friend,
That everybody can depend.
She is a singer, a chef, a writer, a poet,
Name it and she can do it.
You can rely on her end,
Even if you're broken hearted she can mend.

She is really funny,
Surely you will enjoy her company.
She is graceful; she's even full of life's irony,
She can also burst into laughter and cry suddenly,
She is a witty sister and a clever mommy.

Her knowledge in financial literacy is awesome,
You can ask her unendless question,
But never ask for a ransom.
She can advise you on how to save your income,

Because it's her passion, it's her purpose, a true
leader, I wanna become.

My virtual friend, my poetry sister ESTER,
One day, we will sing and dance together,
I hope it is on Easter,
Because it is a memorable day to remember,
A day full of wonder,
More memories to ponder.
Hoping one day, my fighter sister,
Finally, at last!!! We will meet each other.

A PETITE QUEEN

She's a woman with grace,
Petite but you'll love to embrace,
She's a lady full of confidence,
Sweet even a little girl with independence.

She writes so neatly,
And speaks so boldly,
She walks too fast,
That you get furious how she does,
But we always love her anywhere she goes.

She's my dear for a decade or more,
But her charm and wit even grow while she's
getting older,
She became more than knowledgeable of the things
around her,

But still she's sensitive to the people surrounded
her.

She's my JEANNETTE, Lovely to attest,
A brave mother of her own nest,
A patient wife at its best,
Wearing her own crown fit for her till the rest.

JOY...A CHEERFUL FRIEND

I've never seen her long time ago,
But her faces never age and still glow,
I get updated on her through her Facebook
account,
So I know, she's still my friend that I can count.

She's a friend you can lean, tell her all even mean,
She can understand, she's so patient, I've seen,
If you're mad, confront her,
She will give you joy, after all it's her name you'll
enjoy.

When were young she acted boyish, it's alright
she's not selfish,
And now I've seen her wearing skirt, wow she's a
lady but not a flirt. Her simplicity is still there, the
attitude she always care,
The aura remains the same, beauty and brains still
remain.

She will be my forever cheerful friend,
Even we're away and don't chat every day,
Messages and calls are not necessary to extend,
Our hearts bond invisibly and no need to pretend.
I love you forever my JOY. A cheerful friend.

OUR ENGINEER...OUR PRIDE

He is my cousin; he is like a brother and more than
a friend,
He is a pride in our clan, everyone can
comprehend,
He is a real hero to his siblings,
He is the best son to his parents.

Inspite of the degree that he reached,
His humility is still intact no need to teach,
You can always count on him,
He is willing to help, you can trust him.

He can build your home not just a house to live on.
He can design your family's desire so you can rest
peacefully till dawn. He can help you fulfill your

dream while his living on his own realm. He is our pride, he is our engineer, we can all scream.

My dear REVIN, continue to spread love to humanity.
For loving is the key to a successful journey,
But wherever you maybe, share positivity
For it will reflect you and your dignity.
Maintain your peace and serenity.

OUR ACCOUNTANT...OUR BUSINESSWOMAN

She works eight hours a day, workaholic and very
systematic,
She had a lot of sideline business after work, it's
automatic.
She is thrifty, her future is ready,
Properly managed and prepared even her
daughter's sanctuary.

She is our family's accountant, our businesswoman,
A girl with a kind heart and a lady with a loyal
husband,
A woman full of radiance, hope and perseverance.
A mother with so much love and knowledge to
enhance.

Our DIGNA, my aunt, our family's pride,
We love her dearly, no need to hide,

When you need help she can give you a ride,
To life's journey even in a roller coaster tide,
She will be there to help you to cast your side.

She is God fearing, an attitude that she behold,
Resilient to forgiveness, a behaviour she upholds.
You can lean on her, she have stories untold,
To help you think about your future on hold.
Come on, share a life with her and have a forever to fold.

MARYANN, MY WONDERWOMAN

Here she goes, hear ye! hear ye!
My simple friend yet too lovely,
She is MARYANN, my wonder woman.
I'll let you know how incredibly she can become.

She had so many difficulties in her life to run.
But she never gave up, she never quits to her
errands.
Many of her friends left her because gossips she
reprimands.
But now she wanted to show them that she rose up
with head high and hurts no one.

She learned a lot, everyday is a struggle to her.
But she never asks for someone's help,

She never stops believing. You can't see on her face
what she had been. Instead, she smiles at you
hiding and pretending.

I love her because I've seen her good heart when
others can't.
She is a living example of hardship and
blissfulness.
A wonder woman full of courage and strength.
A real woman full of hope and determination.
Someday, all your trials will come to an end.
Keep your faith, Mary Ann, my dear friend.

JOAN LIEZL AND BETTY...MY SISTERS IN THE MOON

I have these two friends; they are both lovely and awesome.
They are both good in businesses; I admired their patience and perseverance. They are both energetic and very responsible.
They are the example of a modern Filipina, totally empowered women, oozing with confidence and talent.

We are thankful we met each other, even in an awkward situation.
We both collided and jive for we possess the same views and principles a decent woman should have.
We never let anyone ruin our friendship because we believe that birds of same feathers flock

together. And even we don't chat regularly, our bond will last forever.

Here's a poem dedicated to both of you,
For believing in me especially in times of blue,
Thank you for a wonderful friendship and sisters we share in hue.
God will bless you always with strength and wisdom to overcome any due.

Remember always that you two are my sisters in the moon,
Giving brighter light to people who's doomed,
Stay your shine and focus on the lighter shades of life, bringing silver linings like those flowers in bloom. I liked your positivity and endurance in all aspects, both of you is in zoom. I love you and we will bond personally too soon.

RAYMOND...MY REAL DIAMOND

I always treated him as my brother, for we speak
the same dialect during our secondary years. We
shared priceless memories, even sometimes with
tears.
He is God-fearing, a good father of the home
possesses
He is hardworking, loyal and nurtures his children
with caresses.

You will be amazed on how he lived his life to the
fullest.
Leaving with traces of humility and integrity at his
best.
Learning from him makes me feel better; he is
sharing his difficulties with laughter. A true
gentleman and a diamond friend, rare to find.

I am proud of his success.

Showing the world about the essence of
perseverance and patience.
In Gods perfect time, he is reaping what he sows
with conscience.
I admire his positivity and strength.
That even he went through many burdens, still
intact with his self-confidence.

He is RAYMOND...my friend, my diamond.
He is a man with a word of honor, principled and
raises his family on his own. Always sparkles in
times of desperation.
Keep on shining bright, your children need your
dedication.
I will see you soon to extend my consolation.
God bless you always and reach your ambitions.

JINKY...AN EXTRA ORDINARY LADY

I met her here in Hongkong, we stayed in the same building.
I know her as a lady with dignity and full of generosity.
A woman with a kind heart, loving and caring.
A bachelorette with high aspirations and dreams for her family.

I never seen her cry even in troubled times
She has enough courage to face uncertainties.
She has wisdom to break the chains of chimes.
I love her company for she shares her positivities.

She has radiance and determination.
She never stops reaching her ambition.
But all of us are waiting for the great celebration.
Where we can hear the churches bell for her wedding dedication.

Her name is JINKY, my happy and extra ordinary
friend.
She has selfless love and upright disposition
I wish you a happy happy birthday with good
intention,
And may God grant all your wishes for a
wonderful life all along.

MY SISTER IN CRIME

To be an only child at home is such a lonely and a
boring world,
But she made it colorful by accompanying me and
sometimes we even played sword, We played
Barbie dolls and be a princess in our blanket made
palace, We run, we jump, we hide, and be merry
till we get tired and when grand mom gets angry at
last.

My childhood memories became more memorable
because of her.
My unforgettable moments became hilarious and
more dramatic that always in my mind lingers. We
rock on the same boat and we even slept together.
She is Lanie, my cousin, my childhood bestfriend,
but I treated her as my sister as we get older. Our
bond became stronger.

Now, she's the best mom of two talented children, so do I,
She's here in Hongkong taking care of a naughty kid, so am I,
She's full of positivity and energy even though many trials came her way, she never gave up, and she stays cheerful and gay.
Do I need to prove my jolliness too, everyday?
I know we're both contented, living a life peacefully and with serenity. She fights for me; she strengthens my ability on how to deal with my insecurities. I lift her up; I share advices on how to manage her differences in this cruel society. She's one of a kind, a helpful sister and a gorgeous daughter,
But don't make her angry, you'll not gonna love to see her.
My dear Lani, focus on your family, uplift your financial stability. And most of all be grateful of what God has given you with humbled heart and good personality.

KERYGEN...MY ENERGEN

I met her here in Hongkong...we came from the
same province, Pangasinan. I hung out before with
her company, we enjoyed taking pictures,
remembrance. We had lots of memorable
experiences, together.
Even shared problems and secrets, unforgettable,
forever.

There was a time she needed to decide, wisely.
Between family or work, passion or money.
Personal career or personal growth.
To family's goal, she needed to choose the truth.

She never regretted what she has been through.
She has full of energy, laughter, like old times do.
And now she's contented with children of two.
A picture of a happy family, she ever wished to
come true.

She is KERYGEN, a lovely queen, our energen.
You can feel in her heart the meaning of a true
friend.
Even we're miles away, she never forgets to pray
for me
She loves me unconditionally even times had
passed away.
I am blessed of having her as a dearly sister, all the
way.

MHEL...OUR PRECIOUS JEWEL

We met at Horizons page, a house where talents
pay homage.
We value respect and we accept different talents
regardless of age. That is why, one day,
A very talented lady came on my way.

Her name is MELBA...Horizons precious jewel.
An awesome woman full of energy and resiliency.
She is our one and only dj, a pride of our
community.
She inspires and motivates others; her way of
reaching them is extraordinary.

We never met personally but our goal binds us
together.
We wanted to help,
Use our voice to raise awareness for uplifting
others.

Her mission is accomplished yet never diminished.

We want to say thank you with a grateful heart.
For giving life to all our masterpieces in your
program, for appreciating our art. We hope and
pray our roads will never be apart.
God bless you always and continue your
advocacies with more power. Horizons family
loves you mam DJ Mhel from the bottom of our
heart.

MY EXUBERANT DAUGHTER

She is my first born, my only daughter,
And I love her dearly and forever,
Everyone knows how hard to be a parent overseas,
But for her brighter future and better tomorrow, I
will conquer all my fears.

I'm at my happiest whenever she is happy,
I'm the saddest whenever she is lonely,
She is energetic, she work dedicatedly for her
savings and extra expenses she pay,
When I'm exhausted, she makes me rest for a day,
by singing her very own melody.

She is a caring sister and a very independent lady.
She is a responsible daughter, very reliable and
friendly.
I pray that she will stay the same especially her
humility.

I'm very proud to be her mother with great
positivity.

My lovely LUCILLE, please do reach your dreams
and build the palace you fit in. Never surrender in
your journeys and walk slowly when the paths are
rocky. Remember to bring your good manners and
always be a God-fearing lady. I will always support
you and even carry you in times of difficulty.
I love you till my last breath takes me away.

MARYANN...AN AWESOME TEACHER

I have a friend that will last till the end.
Her voice is too loud, sometimes alarming.
Makes her students behave, electrifying
But she's nice and friendly, excellent rating.

Her happiness is to ensure her two daughters'
future.
Making sure their behavior is of good character.
Showing them love and giving them proper
nurture.
Leaving life's deepest lesson that makes them
strong like a tiger.

Her name is MARYANN, an awesome teacher.
I salute her for being brave and an excellent
mother.

There may be some misunderstandings along the
way,
Still she continues to fight and gain victory.
She will have more journeys to conquer.
I know she will handle them all in easy manner.

Our friendship is like a diamond.
Shines when needed, sparkles when collided.
We've been a lot, through life's thick and thin.
Our connection is deep from within
I love her till the end.
God bless you my sisterly friend.

JACKELANE...A DIGNIFIED QUEEN

She has this quality that's why other people value her.
She respects others so they treat her with care.
They love her unconditionally even in moments of despair.
She had gone through many battles yet she won them over.

She has sacrificed a lot for her children.
Fought for her life to ensure their safe environment.
Working overseas to save for their future and hopefully can see the results of her endeavor.

She is JACKELANE a dignified queen.
She has her own kingdom fit for her king.
They love each other even not bound in matrimony, they don't bother on this thing. She

believes in love with action rather than the word unseen.

We are friends by the same boat we are rowing.
We are learning together and never stop growing.
We are hoping that tomorrow has always the best thing.
Our life will be an exquisite women empowering and epitome of self-loving we will meet too soon my sweet friend.

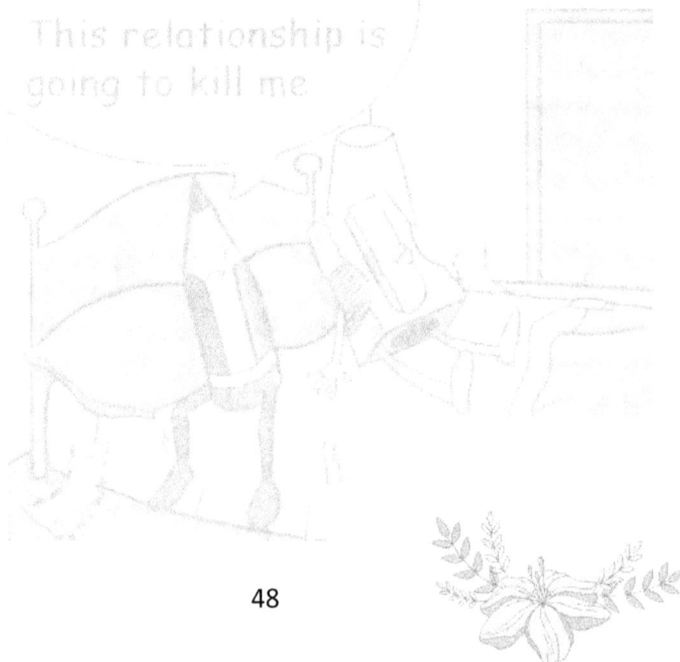

JHODILYN...MY FRONTLINER FRIEND

We lived in the same place before, way back when I
was twenty four,
We were neighbors; we helped each other
especially in household chores. We kept in touch
but only in a little time, we wanted more.
But don't worry my friend, when this pandemic
ends I will be going home to catch up those
moments we missed doing together.

Now, I am here in Hongkong as an OFW, and she's
in the Philippines as BHW, I salute her for being so
active in her chosen career, So tiring and selfless
dedication she needs to endure,
Her responsibility to the community, I am proud of
her and adore.

She is JHODILYN, with two beautiful children, my
frontliner friend,

A true heroine everyone would depend,
I admire her solidarity and resiliency,
Dedication to her responsibility and love of her
country,
A living heroine everyone should be.

May God bless you always with good health to
serve your fellowmen,
A good service that no amount could comprehend,
A true warrior and a wonderful woman in the end,
In your life's journey I will always be here as your
very true friend. I love you and thank you for being
a wonderful human being.

RESTY...MY LOVELY AUNTIE

It was a very long time ago, twenty five years or so.
I don't have a chance to see her but all the good
deeds she did to me I always remember. I have all
the love and respect for her to ponder.
She treated me nicely and care for me like her own
daughter.

She was our neighbor when I was struggling to
survive.
Life was hard for me sometimes I wanted to hide.
But she helped me on her own way so that I can
learn how to survive Slowly but gently she taught
me and now it's my time to show to everyone her
good side.

Her name is ESING for us, a God-fearing woman
and a patient Mom.
Her friends call her RESTY, a lovely auntie in our
community.

She's helpful and jolly, love plants, so many.
She is always humble and cares for the others,
complete integrity.

I may not say these words too often.
But I want to thank you for not allowing me to be
broken.
You are one of the kindest persons.
I truly admire your principles and lessons.
God will always shower His blessings to you
because you deserve a harmonious family.

ROSEGEN...A FLOWER AND A GEM

I've known her way back primary days,
Too long ago but her beauty never fades.
Her honesty and sincerity shows her unique
quality.
Her generosity makes her wealthier.

She is precious like a jade.
Her family needs her, they will never trade.
Her presence is more valuable than any flowers in
their shade.
She's lovely on her own way, a true beauty that will
never fade.

God will always bless you for you are a gem.
A ROSEGEN, wonderful person that everyone
hopes will never change. Stay as humble and as
sweet as you are.

For I adore you and I want to ride one day in your car.

I admired her bravery and strong personality.
She fights for her rights, a decent dignity.
Her success is to see others happy, a very powerful identity.
We love her dearly and wish her a happy, happy birthday.
Pearly, champy and me wishes you all the best and have a wonderful day.

ANALYN...MY EVERGREEN

Our love for each other is as new as it was in the
beginning.
The feeling never changed since we started
knowing.
We are both busy in our chosen fields but we never
missed chatting. Even time has differences we
always share the happiness, smiling.

She works hard so she can travel around the world.
Enjoys her life to the fullest and discover nature
and culture.
She endured a lot of pain when her son battled
from his operation.
Her faith is always intact that makes her stronger
during that difficult situation.

She is a generous friend and a caring sister.

A very thoughtful daughter and a loving mother.
Her simplicity is exemplary that makes her more
beautiful in the eyes of many. Her honesty and
loyalty makes her family closer every day.

Her humility is her behavior that i like most.
Even she has more she never boasts
She is ANALYN, my evergreen; I love her till the
end.
Someday, we will have a time to sit in a bench and
unwind.
We will remember all those memories that we left
behind.

REGIENALD...MY EVERLASTING EMERALD

My only son that brings freshness and vitality to
my spirit, energetic. He has the energy that can
heal my loneliness and homesickness, archaic.
He is like an emerald that embodies unity,
unconditional love and compassion. A stone of
infinite patience and inspiration.

He is a symbol of truth and love
He never hurt my feelings, a blessed gift from
above.
He protects me and he is my shining armour.
I love him that I always pray for his good future
and discover his own self altogether.

He is MARC REGIENALD my future manager.
He has a quiet personality and a sensitive heart that
brings him out of danger He loves to stay at home
and play with his computer
A respectful grandson and a very helpful brother.

I am grateful and blessed of having him in my life
He has always been my shining light
An emerald that I will hold on tight
An everlasting gem that i will treasure all my life.
I love you son and happy, happy birthday from
your ate and me.

MAUREEN...TALENT OVERFLOWING

Her beauty is exceptional; her wit is quick,
unpredictable.
Her exploration is beyond your imagination,
unreachable.
Her talent is overflowing, undeniable.
She is really oozing with charm and grace,
admirable.

She is my sister in poetry, MAUREEN on flame.
I admire her perseverance and patience; her
passion will bring her to fame. She is an artist, poet,
painter, guitarist and a singer, what else can you
name? A multi-talented woman full of courage,
nothing to be ashamed.

A star on her own journey, even she failed many times, she rise up more than a thousand folds. You can learn a lot from life's mystery on her ways, magic on her own stories untold. She is the sweetest person you can behold.
Learn to embrace her beyond what you see, an attitude you can uphold.

I wish her all the best in life for she serves our Lord Almighty with vitality. I love her from the bottom of my heart with respect and honesty.
My mother's friend, what a coincidence, life's own mystery.
A purpose of friendship and a sisterly bond bound to last for century.

JOAN...ARCH OF WISDOM

In our home, she is our one and only auntie
Who will hold you with good character and
positivity
She will boost your morale and share all her
experiences vibrantly
To give you inspiration and look up to life brightly.

I met her virtually yet she gives me all the energy.
My views in life progress as I chat with her anyday
I followed her social media accounts to learn more
about courage and acquire serenity
She is a role model in our society.

She is our auntie JOAN, an arch of wisdom
Her heart is filled with joy, humility and freedom

Free to speak what's on her mind, free from
boredom.
Full of talents that when she shows you, you'll be
out of your mind.

I thanked God I found her and crossed our paths
Learning and growing is not hard when someone
like her will mold you like a lathe I'm praying for
her safety and hoping to meet her someday
Even crossing boarders we are far from each
other...
We will be meeting in Malaysia or any country that
will bring us jolly and gay.

JAYBEE...GENUINE PERSONALITY

We call him our iho mio, for he possesses a
characteristic duo
He can be your brother and she can be your sister,
but he is not confused my big bro! A very humble
person, true friendship beyond your expectation
A genuine personality that is hard to impersonate,
original creation.

A pure heart that loves unconditionally, faithful to
his "mahal", guarantee
A word of honour, he keeps and dignity.
Respectful and just, fulfilling his pledge and duty,
loyalty
He can always lend a helping hand anytime of the
day, humanitarian philosophy.

I appreciate his conduct; he is a noble person,
uprightly.
He has strong moral principles, integrity.

He never boasts even his knowledge is
extraordinary.
Cooking is his passion, excellent taste, the food he
prepares fills my tummy!

He is our iho mio, JAYBEE with a genuine
personality.
Never judge him because we love him dearly
Gods' creation with a freedom to choose his destiny
We will support him in his entire journey
Take care always and we are here in any
difficulties.
We are family.

CHERRY....MIXTURE OF BERRIES

She is a respected teacher, an all-around daughter
She got so many talents and she shares them to us,
her sisters
She embraces life's negativity and turns it into
positivity, alluring power of resiliency. I admire her
for she possesses the smile full of sweetness and
lovely.

She will always lift you up; God's word turns to life
Watch her move in the dance floor, all your worries
be lifted
You will acquire the positive energy she radiates
Every time you see her, a peaceful look on her face
vibrates.

Berries are full of vitamins and nutrients; they are
juicy, round and brightly colored. My sister,
CHERRY is a woman full of wisdom to share,

exuberant and a unique creation to be treasured. I
may not see her personally
But i know deep in my heart she loves me
unconditionally.

Have a cup of berry everyday
Talk with my sister Cherry regularly
Make it a habit and you will see the benefit
Witness in your eyes, body and mind the changes
they will create
Your life will be better and be great!

KENNETH...WIND BENEATH

He is the wind beneath his parents' wings
A brother full of love and care to his siblings
An ambition to be fulfilled for his future realms
A promise of good life and brighter days, he
dreams.

He is JOHN KENNETH, my little brother in poetry
I admire his dedication and loyalty
He is sacrificing a lot just to reach his goals
Even he has poor eyesight; it's not a hindrance to
do his passion
He loves to write, a way to express his emotions.

His intelligence is excellent, scholar, a unique
person
He has the ability to create his own destination,
brilliant creation. I hope you will remember all the
good traits to bring in your journeys, be an
inspiration. Be a good example to our community
and lead them to better direction.

Learn more, change for the best and never stop
growing.
You are our little brother, we love you without
pretending.
I am always praying for your protection and
constant healing, good understanding. Hoping to
meet you also these days that are coming
In the Philippines or in any country that is happy
and exciting!

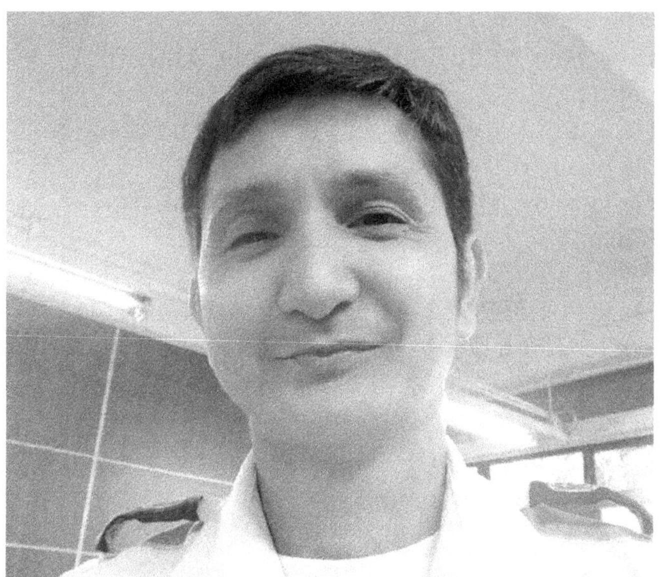

ERIC...THE ICONIC

He is my big brother in poetry, loyal and has a
unique quality.
He is the only one who can make our mami Ody
laugh, a gesture of humor naturally. Very
respectful and extraordinary
His masterpieces are really from the bottom of his
heart and deep vocabulary.

I found him awesome because of his experiences in
his life
He shares them sometimes and you can really learn
a lesson to be your guide
A gentleman and a very responsible husband
A dignified father and a very loving son.

He works hard for his children's future

Even he is petite his heart is big and caring in
nature
He is always on the right track, you cannot judge
his behavior
He knows well what to say and do, a man with
honor.

He is kuya ERIC, horizons pride and unico iho
We love him dearly for his honesty and integrity
Take care always for God will provide all your
needs
I hope to meet you soon, my kuya Eric, the Iconic.

BAMBEE...OUR HONEYBEE

She is the one and only Daniw Princess in the
world of poetry
I was amazed by the way she writes deep Ilokano
dialect, really extraordinary
She has enchanting words and magical poems that
will lead you to a paradise. A day reading her
daniws will make you mesmerize
A woman with wisdom you will realize.

She is sweet and always ready to help you
I have proven her humility many times never due
She has a lot of experiences to share in her
masterpieces
Still intact with her faith and belief inspite of life's
difficulties.

I respect her for her ability to go with the life's flow,
adaptive

She is sacrificing here in other country just to give a better life to her family, productive. She is a loyal member of different organizations here in Hongkong, friendly and interactive. She is a softball player, very energetic and active.

Her name is BAMBEE, honeybee in our home
Sweet as candy, lively on her tone
I am always inspired of her ability and creativity.
A woman symbolizing power and strong personality.
I love you always my ate Bambee.

EVELYN...MY HONGKONG BESTFRIEND

A woman with good character and strength
Embodies loyalty and never quits on life's
difficulties, very resilient
She's petite but her heart is bigger than the
universe
You can see her smile and full of positivity even in
times of adversity.

I love her points of view
A God fearing lady who always sees the silver
linings, behind the rainbow Sunshine radiates on
her face
In times of despair, she was my solace.

Her name is EVELYN, my Hongkong Bestfriend
She never left my side and always believes in me
'till the end
She never doubted on me and we are learning
together

Our life's story is always a lesson to ponder.

A girl full of dreams and hopes
Stay as you are and maybe one day, destiny will
change your horoscope I am just one chat away my
dear sister
God will always bless you with love so tender
I love you and thank you for being my best
photographer
Now, you all know who took my wonderful
pictures...□

MAMI SOL...WOMAN WITH GOOD SOUL

I call her mami in our home talent sweet home
Her beauty is ageless, fountain of youth
Her gracefulness reflects on her dance moves
She will guide you and always help you to know
the truth.

She is an epitome of woman empowerment
A leader of different organizations and
humanitarian missions
Love of country she embodied with compassion
She is a very talented woman and resilient to
different situation.

I admire her dedication and loyalty to our country

Even in overseas she helps our kababayans, salute
to her act of humanity Kindness from the bottom of
her heart exudes brightly
Shining on her face that makes her more pretty
An elegant woman of society.

She is my mami SOL a woman with good soul
I congratulate her for sharing her talents to create
positivity and not turmoil I thank her for being my
second mother in poetry
She really inspires me especially on her cooking
ability.
God bless you always my dearest mami...

ZENY...OUR WONDERFUL MAMI

She is Horizons pride, loyalty and her dedication
you can derive
One of the amazing mothers in the world of poetry
A reason how I found this home of literacy.

Her kitchen from Canada always added spice in
our home talent sweet home If you're full, your
mind won't write something that will bring you to
doom You can write about happiness and
contentment, love and forget resentment Thank
you, Mami ZENAIDA for making us full everyday,
it brings us good compliments.

Her beauty is undeniable, her dedication to our
country is unforgettable She helped a lot of our
kababayans during her stay here in Hongkong She
shares her talents and use it for preserving our
culture for the next generation. I am so lucky to be

one of her daughters in this world full of
contradictions.

Her compassion and kindness gave her success
A true royalty with the grace she possesses
She is a wonderful woman to her children, forever
they are blessed
I am hoping to be with you soon my Mami dearest
Horizons family loves you and we are always
praying for your best.

MILDRED... BEAUTIFUL INDEED

Cousin by blood, sister by heart
Our connection is strong, we will never depart
A loving mother and a caring sister
Her green thumb exploded in her garden,
everywhere blooming with beautiful flowers.

She is always ready to fight for me
Can lean on her especially in time of adversity
I believe on her abilities and admire her energy
Even she is petite she radiates positivity.
Her heart is bigger than anyone would be.

Her name is MILDRED... Beautiful woman, indeed.
Don't make her mad or else your dead!
She's jolly yet sensitive, we played a lot, even
braids my thin long haired.

I always smile whenever I remember her

She's sweet and comfortable to be with.
In her company, you'll never be blue
Days and nights will be bright because of you
My Mildred, I love you!

JANE LYN... TRULY AMAZING

I saw her face with a beautiful smile
That captivated my heart even we're apart by miles
We started chatting with a simple hello
Knowing her is knowing an angel with an invisible
halo.

She's an inspiration to many
Uplift your morale and helps overcome worry
Undeniably gorgeous, an amazing lady
A compassionate leader with an exuberant
personality.

Her name is JANE LYN, truly an amazing woman
Everybody knows her with exceptional brilliance
Her existence is admiration and testimony
That life is a never-ending lessons journey.

Continue to be a peace ambassadress
Spread your wings of love and genuine humility

For the world needs a real one like you
To unites goals and heal broken hearts
For unity and for equality.

JOAN...VERY CREATIVE MIND

She is our new sister in our home, Horizons.
A very talented lady in bloom
She discovered her talent in writing in their class
We welcomed and embraced her in our house
We are all amazed on how fast she could adjust
Admirable person to last!

She is the one responsible to our beautiful posters
at home
Very creative and patient, wide imagination
She loves to make desserts and one day, I hope i
can taste and take some at home
My lovely sister we will bond soon.

I encouraged her to write more and never stop
doing her passion
I could see myself to her when I also began in this
organization

I believe she got talent and magical hands on her
creations
We are blessed and grateful of having you here at
Horizons
We hope you learn more and we grow together
leading to our great destination Hand in hand, we
can do this together!

Her name is JOAN, a lady with a very creative
mind.
Thank you for your loyalty and dedication, you
never leave us behind
A real sister with a humbled heart and
humanitarian mission
God bless you always and continue doing your
happiness in this home Fulfill your dreams and
ambitions.

MY "CHUBBY" FRIEND

JOAN is her name,
Direct to the point no more guessing game,
When we are just sweet sixteen,
Her body is really "chubby" not so thin.

I guess eating is her hobby,
No one dare to query,
She will get upset and angry,
If you try to stop and take the food away
But she said it's not true, she just eats a little
everyday.

She's sweet like her candies,
Caring like her teddies,
Funny like her gummies,
She's awesome like her fresh bake cookies.

My dear Joan, don't you worry,
In today's genre, "chubby" is the new sexy,

We are very proud of having you in our group,
Because you make our days always happy and gay.

Stay sweet and we love you dearly,
Our friendship is one in a million stories,
Can keep for eternity,
Can show to humanity.
We love you from the bottom of our "body".

FAYE...MY SISTER GRAY

I consider her as my virtual sister, for she upholds a sister like character. I will chat her in times of my despair; she listens and helps me to repair. She makes me laugh, shares her joy and we enjoy relaxing together. That's why I call her my sister gray because she has her balance and neutrality, an attitude that transcend her day by day.

Her work regularly surpasses all expectations,
Being a faithful wife and a caring mother beyond limitations,
Taking her responsibilities with full hearted dedication,
A promise that she fulfills with her everyday obligation.

Her real name is HANNAH FAYE but I prefer her nickname Faye, my sister colored gray. Gray is an intermediate color of black and white, like her, a perfect neutral person of dark and bright. Don't make her angry you'll see her face get dark, just make her happy so she'll be merry and bright. Her happiness is her two gorgeous girls, never lose her attention, they are always on her sight.

She likes to travel and I'm looking forward of touring around with her. We like to eat and I would like to have lots of crab to share with.
We have a lot of common traits, an inspirational woman possess.
And I love her dearly even in virtually, only we caress.
Take good care of yourself and stay safe don't be careless.
God bless you always and thank you for a wonderful friendship and sisters we attest.

BUDDY

She was my "buddy",
We are mates and sometimes we almost have the
same hobby,
We are close and we often stay in the lobby,
To watch students do their own activity.

Now we are aged,
Have our own family and we finish our own rage,
Still our friendship locked in the cage,
And bonded to last not to fade.

CHARO is her name,
Sweet, lovely and tame,
Now she feels like a winner in the game,
Because she's living a life, full of comfort and fame.

One day, when this pandemic stop,
We will bond and go to shop,
We will eat nonstop for we are craving our favorite
ice cream on top,

And that day will be the happiest day our
friendship could have.

Someday, our roads will cross again,
We will reminisce the days and remember lessons
that we gain, Forgetting the pain,
And embracing life's blessing, and our friendship
in our hearts will always remain.

THE BACHELORETTE

I have a little secret; I don't wanna talk about it
But if you insist, i will share a bit
It's all about my friend way back nineteen ninety
seven
She is not yet married up to this time; maybe she
thought she's just eighteen
Hello, my dear! We're road to forty next weekends.

She travels around the world using her magic
wallet
Oh no! She met a prince with a magic carpet
It's not a literal carpet, but a man from Egypt
I guess that's our little secret.

We're all waiting for the church's bells

On that day we will be filled with joy and we will
celebrate 'til we fall asleep with gladness,
For at last you are under his spell.

Oh my dear, XENIA don't be late like the first letter
of your name,
Almost near the last alphabet, don't be ashamed
Enjoying one's freedom is admirable, but age is also
a matter
Especially at this time, where we need comfort and
power.
Be like princess Jasmin who lived with her prince
happily ever after.

TESTIMONY

Your love for me is incomparable
Annoying you each day is almost impossible
But things work out well
Because of your patience and understanding
I can attest it's incredible!

Having you in my life is unexpected
Never thought of being with someone so dedicated
Loyalty and gentleness make me more finesse
I always want to feel you in my senses.
I can witness your faithfulness!

Being in love with someone
Is the most exciting part of our journey
We will experience downs and victory

Nevertheless it's a part of our story
To be a living proof that God exists especially in
times of difficulty I will still love you and choose
you
I can say this is a testimony!

This love i felt for you changed my perceptions
Unforgettable moments never deceived my
expectations
You changed my life into a joyous one
Have proven that life is like a rosary, full of
mystery
Yet adventure never ends in misery
Always a happy ending because of your love
that is eternity!
From my heart it's infinity!

I love you.
I will always do
Forever grateful that we belong and found each
other
Never regretted those days that is wasted
More years waiting for our love to be bonded
Nurturing with compassion
Love with trust and genuine intention
I know you're my soulmate and my affirmation!

PANGALAN

Ang tawag sa akin
Nang mga guro, kaklase at kaibigan
Ay "Annaliza", talaga namang magandang
pangalan
Ibinigay at inisip ng aking mga magulang
Hango sa teleseryeng sikat noong kanilang
kapanahunan.

Sa aming tahanan at sa aking malalapit na kaibigan
"Liezle" ang kanilang sambit tuwing ako'y
kailangan
Pero ng ako'y nangibang bayan
"Anna" o "Liza" naman kung ako'y bansagan.

Kahit alin diyan sa mga nabanggit
Ay pwedeng sa akin isambit
Sapagkat ako nama'y madaling lapitan

Kaibigan na pwedeng asahan
At kapatid na madaling lapitan.

Ano man ang ating pangalan
May kaniya-kaniya tayong katangian
Hubugin at linangin
Para sa ikakabuti ng ating katauhan.

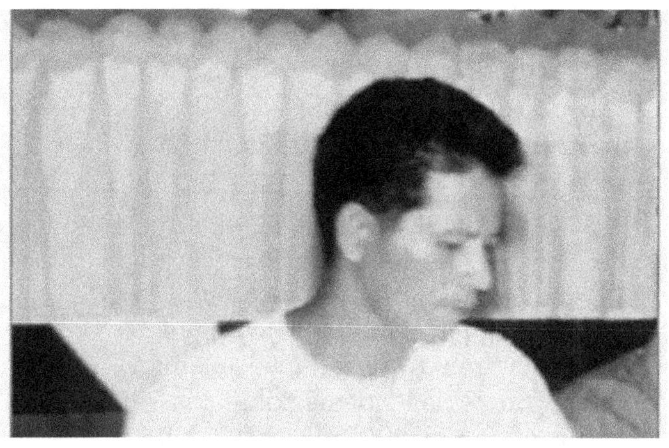

TULA PARA SA AMING AMA

Para sa haligi ng aming tahanan, ANACLETO ang pangalan
Na maagang lumisan at kami ay iniwan
Alam kong nasaan ka man ngayon, kami ay pagmasdan,
Na magkaroon ng pagkakataong magkakilanlan
At sa loob ng dalawampu't taong nakaraan
Kaming lahat ay nasa mabuting kalagayan.

Ikaw na aming ama, na nagkaroon ng anim na anak,
Iba-iba man ang pinagmulan at kami'y watak-watak,
Subalit kami sa inyo ay humahanga at pumapalakpak,
Sapagkat kami ay may pagkakaisa at ang aming mga buhay ay matiwasay na tinatahak.

Hindi mo man nadama ang aming pagmamahal

At nagawa sa inyo ang mga tungkulin,
Bilang mabuting anak at ibigay ang lahat ng
inyong naisin,
Pero kami ay nangangako na aming gagawin at
tutuparin
Ang mga pangarap na nais ninyo para sa amin.

Aming ama, malayo ka man sa amin,
Alam naming payapa ka at nakatingin,
Sa bawat tagumpay ay kasama ka namin,
At balang araw kami ay magkikita kita din,
Matutupad ang matagal mo ng tagubilin.
Mahal ka namin ama, salamat sa pamanang sining.

Inspirasyon namin sa panulat ang aming ama
Ang panganay at bunsong anak sa kanya nagmana

ANG KAIBIGAN KONG DE KAMPANILYA

Sa talino at tapang hindi mo matatawaran,
Kapag ikaw ay nagkasala sa batas, tiyak ika'y
walang kapatawaran,
Siya ang kaibigan kong "attorney" kung aming
turingan,
Pero "MISHIELE ATANGAN" talaga ang kaniyang
pangalan.

Kaibigan ko siya, dekada na ang nakalipas,
Pero ang kaniyang ganda, wala pa ding kupas,
Dumagdag pa ang kaniyang tayong matikas,
Kapag siya ay nagtanong tiyak wala ka ng takas.

Ang mga katulad niya ay ingatan nating tunay,
Sapagkat minsan ka lang makakahanap ng
kaibigang walang kapantay,
At maasahan pang habang buhay,
Sana pwedeng libre ang serbisyo kung kapitbahay.

Salamat sa'yo kaibigang de kampanilya,
Dahil sa'yo kampante kaming talaga,
Na may magtatanggol sa amin para makalaya,
Sa tanikalang kami din ang nakagawa.

NAPAGTAGUMPAYANG PAGSUBOK

Ako'y may nakilala, nagmula sa malayong
probinsiya,
"ALTHEA" ang pangalan at talagang masayahin
siya,
Mababakas mo sa mukha niya ang kaligayahan,
Tahimik niyang kalooban ang aming napag-
usapan.

Ako ay nagulat sa mga nadinig ko,
Kwento ng buhay niya'y tiyak na may aral na
ginto,
Siya ang babaing hindi sumuko,
Sa kahit anong unos na dumaan dito.

Siya ay babaing palaban, naturan ko na lang,

Sa tibay ng loob at talas ng isipan,
Lahat kinaya niya at napagtagumpayan,
Sa tulong na din ng Diyos na makapangyarihan.

Napagtanto ko ng landas nami'y maghiwalay,
Napakapalad niya at may mapagkumbabang
pusong taglay,
Na kahit ano man ang kaniyang pinagdaanan,
Natutunan pa din niyang magmahal sa kabila ng
kahirapan.

Sana ay palagi siyang gabayan ng Panginoon
Hanggang sa marating niya ang pangarap niyang
paroroonan.
Diyos nawa ang sumama at gagabay sa kanya
Yan ang panalangin ko sa mga darating pang
pagsubok sa buhay niya
Kahit alam ko namang kayang-kaya niya!

LAW SIN KYU

Kagaya ng mga ibon sa iyong likuran,
Darating ang panahon na ika'y aking iiwan,
Para humanap ng bagong kapalaran,
Kung saan makikita ang bagong kinabukasan.

Saan man ako mapadaan,
Mananatili ka sa puso ko magpakailanman,
Ikaw ang nagsilbing pangalawa kong tahanan,
Ako'y magiging pangalawang ina mo
magpasawalang hanggan.

Ng ako'y dumating, ikaw ay isang taon lang,
Wala pang muwang, pero ngayon, napakarami ng
nalalaman.
Sa ngayon, ikaw ay siyam na taong gulang,
nakakatuwang pagmasdan,
Na ang munting anghel ko nuon, ngayon ay isa
nang katibayan ng aking kasipagan.

Oh, aking KyuKyu, ako ay lilisan,
Sa darating na Disyembre ng taong kasalukuyan,
Huwag kang malumbay at mag-alinlangan,
Ikaw ay mananatiling nakaukit sa puso ko at
isipan.

AUGUSTO...ANG KAIBIGAN KONG HENYO

Ang pagiging henyo ay ano nga ba para sa inyo?
Ito ba ay ang mga nakapagtapos ng mga may
gradong uno?
O sila ba ang mga taong dumiskarte ng todo?
O dili kaya ang mga nilalang na may angking
kakaibang galing at talento.

Ang kaibigan ko, alam ko, isa siyang henyo!
Pagdating sa talas ng isipan, hindi papatalo.
Kung sumagot sa mga tanong ay hindi pabiro,
Pero lahat ay kapupulutan ng aral sa mundo.
Henyo siya, sa paraan at paniniwalang alam ko.

Siya ay si AUGUSTO TALAUE, JR kumpletong
pangalan niya ito

105

Kagaya rin niya ang mga anak niyang minamahal
na totoo.
Ang asawa niya at buong pamilya, siya ay idolo.
Ikinakarangal nila at pinagmamalaki sa buong
mundo.

Si kaibigan Agosto, malayo pa ang lalakbayin.
Pero alam Kong pangarap niya kayang-kaya
niyang dalhin.
Sapagkat ang pananampalataya niyang taimtim,
Ang siyang nagdala sa kanya sa ganiyang layunin.
Ipagpatuloy nawa niya ang pagiging maawain.
Salamat, sa mga aral na kanyang hinabilin.

DIANA...AMERIKANANG NEGRA

Marahil para sa inyo, ito ay titulong kakaiba.
Pero sa aming pamilya, 'yan ang bansag na maganda.
Tawag ni lolo sa pinsan kong sopistikada,
Dahil sa kulay niyang taglay na kanilang kinukutya.

Noong kami ay mga bata pa, kilalang-kilala siya.
Kulay ng balat niya ay namana niya sa kaniyang ama.
Pero iyan ang bagay niya para maging kapansin-pansin siya, Napaka mahinhin at mahiyaing bata.

Siya si pinsan DIANA, may dalawang anak at asawa'y mapagpakumbaba.
Sila'y tahimik at payapa, tanggap ang kahinaan ng bawat isa.

Nagsisikap para mapalaki ang mga anak ng
maayos at sagana.
Hindi alintana ang sasabihin ng iba.

Wala sa kulay o katayuan sa buhay.
Nasa pagkatao at nilalaman ng puso ang
tagumpay.
Nasa pakikipag-kapwa tao na siya namang
kaniyang taglay.
Kinagigiliwan naming siyang tunay.
Diana, ang prinsesa sa aming buhay.

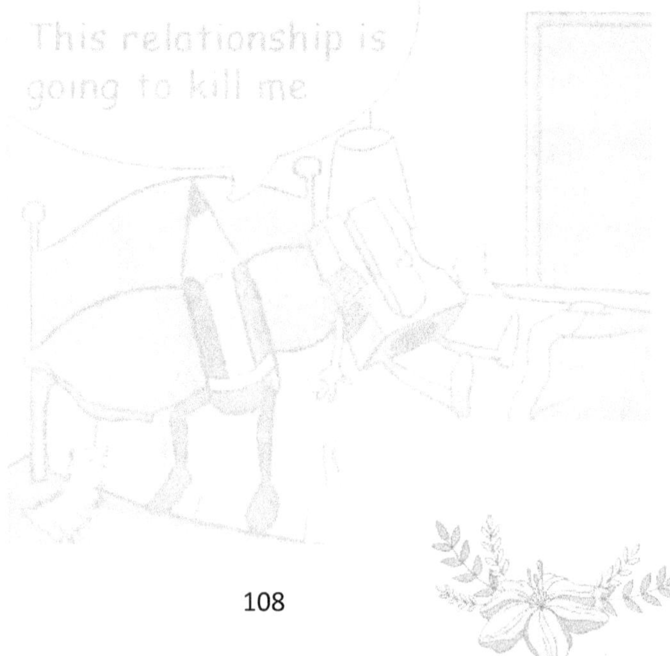

JOVY...ANG KAIBIGAN KONG GROOVY

Masaya siyang kalaro noong kami ay mga bata pa.
Marami kaming masasayang ala-ala.
Isa siya sa aking mga kababata na palagi kong
kakutsaba
Kay lolo at lola magpapaalam para ako ay
makagala.

Napakaliksi at napakasipag niya.
Tunay na kaligayahan makikita sa kaniyang
mukha.
Kahit mahirap ang kaniyang buhay kanya itong
kinakaya.
Para sa mga anak na napakahalaga sa kaniya.

Kahit anong klase ng trabaho ay papasukan niya.
Maitaguyod lamang ng maayos ang kaniyang
pamilya.
Matulungin na anak at mapagmahal na ina.

Masipag na kapatid at tapat na asawa.

Siya ay si JOVY, ang kapitbahay kong groovy.
Kababata ko na pingat kung aming bansagan.
Sapagkat sa tawa niyang malakas, ako ay
mapapabalikwas.
Siya ay masayahin, grooving sa bawat araw na
dumating.

Magalang at matuwid
Pero para ding leon kung magalit
Aawayin ang sino mang nasa maling panig
Kaya mag-ingat ka sa kaniyang salitang malupit.
Para makaiwas ka sa kaniyang hagupit.

Sa mga panalangin ko, palagi ay kasama siya.
Na sana ay huwag siyang magbabago sa pagiging
mapagpakumbaba.
Sana ay darating din ang kanyang ginhawa.
Manalig at magtiwala nawa sa Diyos Ama na may
Likha.
At mabigyan kami ng pagkakataong magkita.

CIPRIANO...ANG AKING SUPERHERO

Siya ay walang taglay na kapangyarihan,
Gaya ng ibang "superhero" na ating kinagigiliwan.
Pero dinaig niya ang karamihan
Sapagkat binago at muling kinulayan ang buhay
ko.

Siya ay si CIPRIANO, pero JHONG kung siya ay
tawagin.
Malayo man siya sa piling ko, pero pag-ibig niya ay
nadarama ko.
Pagmamahal niya'y walang kupas, kahit minsan
ako ay pasaway ng wagas.

Inuunawa niya ako dahil alam niyang puso ko pa
din ang magwawagi.
Kami din ay magkakasama sa huli.

Mahirap man ang aming kalagayan,
Sa magkabilang mundo kami ay nananahan.
Mananaig ang pagtitiyaga at pagtitiis,
Mga kapangyarihang taglay ng pusong umiibig.
Dahil sa aming pagmamahal an, amin itong
mapagtatagumpayan.

Siya ang aking superhero,
Lakas at tibay ng loob, sa kaniya'y hinuhugot ko.
Kasama ng mga anak na inspirasyon ko,
Sila ang talagang bumubuo ng pagkatao ko.
Salamat sa pamilyang mayron ako,
Tunay na kayamanan sa buhay ko.

MILA...DAKILANG INA

Marami sa atin ang may kinikilalang dakila.
Tulad nang kaibigan kong isang napakagandang
halimbawa.
Nang tunay na pagpapahalaga at paghubog ng
isang mapayapang pamilya.
Pagmamahalang hindi kukupas at pagsasama
hanggang wakas.

Siya ang pinakatahimik kong kaibigan, mahinhin
na dapat tularan.
Kapag araw ng paghinga, magsisimba at
magpapasalamat sa lahat ng biyaya.
Mas nanaising mapag-isa kaysa sumama sa mga
grupong magpahamak sa kaniya.
Ang pagtawag sa naiwang pamilya sa Pilipinas ay
sapat na para mairaos ang araw ng pahinga.
Masaya na, nakatipid pa!

Siya ang aking ate MILA, na isang dakilang ina.
Hindi nagsasawa sa paggabay sa mga anak niya.

Kapupulutan ng mabuting aral ang mga kuwento
niya
Isa rin siyang halimbawa ng mapagpakumbabang
kapatid at asawa.

At ngayon, sa araw ng kaniyang kaarawan.
Simple lamang ang kaniyang mga kahilingan.
Makapagtapos ng pagaaral ang kaniyang mga anak
ang tunay niyang kaligayahan. Nagsusumikap at
nagtitiis sa ibang bansa para sa kanilang
kinabukasan. Balang araw ay uuwing bitbit an
tagumpay na inaasam-asam.
Maligayang kaarawan, malapit ko na siyang
maging ninang.
Salamat sa lahat ng aming pinagsamahan.

ALBERT...ANG KAIBIGAN KONG EXPERT

Eksperto siya sa lahat ng bagay,
Pero sa pambobola sa mga kababaihan, siya ay sablay.
Siya ang tumulong sa aking anak,
Nang isali niya ito sa isang patimpalak.
Mula noon, unti-unting napagtagumpayan ang daang tinahak.
Hindi ko makakalimutan at nais magpasalamat
S pamamagitan ng tulang ito kahit na payak.

Matulungin siyang tunay, ugaling palagi niyang isinasabuhay.
Sa kaniyang grupong itinatag, may dedikasyon at napakasipag
Maaasahan kahit anong oras siya tawagan.
Palabiro man pero isang totoong tao at kaibigan.

Siya ay si ALBERT, ang kaibigan kong expert.
ATOK kung tawagin ng kaniyang mga kasama.

Sa pag-awit man o pakikipag kapwa tao at
pakikisama siya ay palaging handa.
Walang reklamo kahit na pagod basta may
pagkaing nakahanda.
Sa kaniyang paguwi, ang anak at asawa pati na ang
alagang aso ang kaniyang ligaya.

Salamat sa kanya, tunay siyang mapagpakumbaba.
Sa mga aral na naibahagi sa akin at sa iba.
Patunay siyang may mga mabubuting tao na
huwaran ng iba
Handang maglingkod sa kapwa at tagasunod ni
Bathala
Sana ay madami pa ang maging kagaya niya
Malapit na kaming magkitang muli ng aking kuya.

RONNIE...ANG TITO KONG POGI

Siya ang paborito kong tito, huwag ng magselos
ang iba dahil nadama ko kasing mahal niya akong
talaga.
Sa tuwing papasyal ako sa bahay nila, madami
siyang pabaon sa akin, para akong bata kung
tratuhin.
Kahit mahirap ang buhay mas uunahin ang iba
kaysa sarili.
Masipag sa trabaho para maitaguyod ang buong
pamilya, kahangahangang ugaling mayron siya.

Maunawain at madiplomasiyang magsalita.

Mahinahon at magaling makisama.
"Richard" ang tawag nila sa kaniya dahil siguro sa kagwapuhan niya.
"Master" naman ang bansag ng mga barkada niya dahil siguro sa abilidad niya.

Ang tito kong pogi ay ang nag-iisang si RONNIE.
Sa buong pamilya namin siya ang katangi-tangi.
Lahat ay ginagalang siya at pinupuri.
Dahil sa pakikisamang tunay na walang pag-aatubili.

Salamat sa lahat ng aral na kanyang ibinahagi.
Palagi kong natatandaan ang kanyang pagiging mabuti.
Pinagdarasal ko ang kanyang kalusugan parati.
Sana ay dagdagan pa ang mga video niya sa tiktok
Para ako ay may mapanood bago magpahinga sa gabi.
Mahal ko talaga ang tito kong pogi.

ANGELICA...ANGHEL SA LUPA

Kami ay magkapatid sa ama
At magkaiba man ang aming mga ina
Kami ay pinagbubuklod sa bahay ng literatura
Magkalayo man kami ng bansa.

Hindi pa man kami nagkikita mula pagkabata
Sa puso ko, may dapat akong ibahagi sa kaniya
Mga aral sa buhay na dapat niyang madala
Para sa ika-uunlad at ika-aangat ng buhay niya.

Isang batang may pangarap
Kasing taas man ng alapaap, siya ay nagsusumikap
Isang taon na lang at siya na ang lilipad
Patungo sa tagumpay na bunga ng kanyang
pagsisikap.

Si ANGELICA...siya ay anghel sa lupa
Pagbuklorin niya sana ang ating pamilya

Para sa ikakatuwa ni ama
Na sa bawat sandali ay inalalayan ka
Para marating ang buhay na maginhawa
Palagi lamang akong andito bilang ate niyang
nakatatanda.

NIÑA...KAIBIGAN KONG MAGANDA

Ang tunay na kagandahan ay nasa panloob na
katauhan
Wala sa panlabas na kaanyuan
Pero itong aking kaibigan
Sa loob at sa labas ay may angking kagandahan.

Siya ay aking kaklase noong sekondarya
Hanggang ngayon ay kaibigan kong dakila
Pinagpala ng Poong Maykapal dahil may buhay na
masaya
Payapa at tahimik, sa bansang Dubai siya ay
nakatira.
Kasama ang mabait na asawa
Sana pagkaroon ng anak ay mabiyayaan sila.

Siya ay si MARIA NIÑA...kaibigan kong maganda.
Hanggang ngayon ay hindi nagbabago ang itsura
at postura
Higit sa lahat, matulongin sa kapwa

Mahilig magtanim at nageeksperimento ng luto
Buti na lang at puro masasarap ang kinalalabasan
nito.

Panalangin ko sana ay huwag siyang magbabago
Kababaang loob at kabutihang taglay nito
Siyang tunay na nagdadala ng kaniyang tagumpay
Sana darating ang araw na magkita kami
Upang magkuwentuhan sa artistahing binibini.

GEMMA....BINIBINING MAKATA

Nang ako ay pumasok sa mundo ng literatura
Ako ay nahiwagaan sa misteryosong "profile" niya
Dalawang mata na tila nangungusap
Kapag nagkomento, lalabas ang mga
makabuluhang pangungusap.
Napukaw niya ang aking atensyon, at nabuhayang
muli ang pangarap.

Napahanga akong talaga sa talas ng kaniyang
isipan
Sa wikang Filipino hindi matatawaran
Ang kaniyang galing at bilis, saan mang larangan
Kung sasabak tiyak ang gantimpalang
makakamtan.

Siya ang aming ate GEMMA...nag-iisang binibining
makata.
Ang titulong para lamang sa kaniya

Koronang kailanman ay hindi maagaw ng iba
Dahil ang kaniyang istilo ay bukod tanging talaga,
Nag-iisang prinsesa ng wika.

Dalangin kong sana'y huwag siyang magbabago
Kababaang loob at may mabuting puso
Handang tumulong sa mga baguhang kagaya ko
Patuloy na inspirasyon sa mundong ginagalawan
ko.
Panatilihin ang malinis na hangarin sa bahay ng
mga talentado.

TATAY PIANONG COLUMBINO

Sa nag-iisang tatay ng aming tahanan
Dalangin namin sa Amang makapangyarihan
Na sana kayo po ay palaging gabayan
Araw-araw na magkaroon ng malakas na
pangangatawan.

Salamat po sa inyong gabay
Mga aral na itinuro sa aming buhay
Sa ugaling walang makakapantay
Napakagaling makisama at matiising tunay.

Mapagpakumbaba at may takot sa Diyos
Mga pamanang ikinalulugod naming lubos
Salamat po sa pagmamahal na tunay
May pusong ginintuan sa paglalakbay sa buhay.
Salamat po, aming tatay.

Ngayong kaarawan mo

Sana ay masaya kang totoo
Pagpalain at ipagkaloob mga kahilingan niyo
At madami pa pong pagdiriwang ang darating na
kasama kayo.

Maligayang kaarawan aming tatay
Mula sa mga anak niyo, mahal kayong tunay
Panalangin ang tangi naming maibibigay
At pasasalamat po sa pagbibigay niyo sa amin ng
buhay
Happy happy happy birthday po tatay

RODELYN...ILOKANANG MAGALING

Siya ay nakilala ko sa bahay ng Horizons
Natulala ako sa galing na taglay nito
Ang mga akda niya ay kamangha-manghang talaga
Mula sa puso, gamit ay malalalim na salita.

Tagos sa kaibuturan ng aking pagkatao
Tuwing babasahin ko mga panulat ng ate ko
At nang siya ay nakasama at nakakuwentuhan ko
Abah! Isang ilokanang pinagpala at napaka elegante pala nito.

Isang inang huwaran, mga anak napag-aral na may karangalan
Magandang halimbawa sa ating lipunan
Mapagpakumba sa kabila ng angking kagalingan

Talaga namang aking kinagigiliwan.

Sa panulat siya ay si "shadesnpens"
Isang alyas na talagang nakakapukaw ng pansin
Lahat ng kaniyang akda ay may hatid na leksyon
Mga aral sa buhay na magagamit nating
proteksiyon.

Akin talagang pinagpapasalamat
Na nagkrus ang aming landas
Isang ate na matatag at idolo ko sa panulat
Sana ay huwag magbabago at palaging may lakas.
Ate kong RODELYN tunay na pinagmamalaki ng
mga ilokanang kagaya namin.

RISTE...PUNO NG DISKARTE

Isa sa mga kapitbahay na aking naging inspirasyon
Sa pagsuong sa mga hamon sa buhay ng may
determinasyon
Tibay at lakas ng kaniyang kalooban
Talaga namang aking hinahangaan.

Isa sa aking naging kaagapay
Sa mga panahong napakalungkot ng buhay
Maraming aral ang aming hinimay-himay
Lahat aming kinaya at nakamit ang tagumpay.

Ngayon ay nabubuhay na ng tahimik at matiwasay
Isang halimbawa ng babaeng may magandang
disposisyon sa buhay Hindi nawalan ng pag-asa
bagkus ay nanalangin ng taimtim
Hindi inalintana ano man ang sabihin ng iba na
puro paninimdim

Dahil naniniwalang magliliwanag din lahat ng
dilim.

Ang aking ate RISTE...punong-puno ng diskarte
Ang kaniyang buhay ay may magandang mensahe
Ito ay tula ng pasasalamat
Ang buhay kong ito ay umangat
Dahil sa kanya, nagpatuloy ako sa aking mga
pangarap
Balang araw, maabot ko din ang alapaap.

NEMYLOU...MAY MAPAGPAKUMBABANG PUSO

Sa wakas ay dumating na ang nakatakdang araw
Na ikaw, aking kapatid sa panulat ay maalayan
Ng isang tulang akma sa iyong katauhan
Isang tula na rin para ikaw ay pasalamatan.

Salamat at ikaw ay nakilala ko
Sa bahay na puno ng mga talentado
Isa ka sa taong inidolo at hinangaan ko
Mula ng ako ay pinapasok sa inyong bahay kubo.

Ang mga akda mo ay napakaganda at
napakagaling
Hinabi at ginawa kasama ng iyong puso at utak na
magaling
Kamangha-mangha at talaga namang lahat ay
napapailing
Sa husay at lalim, tunay kang nagniningning.

Kaya naman nagsikap akong matuto

Dahil isa kang gabay at pamantayan ko
Ang mga narating mo noon at natamo
Ay tunay ngang sumasalamin sa pagiging
manunula mo.

Ako ay nagsimulang muli, at ikaw ang naging
inspirasyon
Tunay na nagpabago at nagbigay sa akin ng
dedikasyon
Naramdaman ko ang iyong kababaang loob
Mga matatamis mong ngiti, makapalagayang loob
Salamat, ikaw ay tunay kong kinararangal. Salamat
at isa kang tunay na kapatid dito sa bahay
Sana ay ipagpatuloy ang sa akin ay paggabay.

LUCITA...MAPAGMAHAL NA INA

Salamat po aking mama
Sa buhay na ibinigay mong biyaya
Walang makakapantay ng iyong ginagawa
Sa akin at sa ating buong pamilya.

Salamat po aking mama
Sa pagsasakripisyo mo sa ibang bansa
Sa lahat ng kabutihang aking natutunan
Binaon ko lahat ng iyong tinuran
Sa pakikibaka sa buhay na puno ng
pakikipagsapalaran.

Salamat po aking mama
Sa pamanang pusong mapagpakumbaba
Sa buhay kong puno ng kulay
Ikaw ang palagi kong kaagapay.
May takot sa Diyos at matulunging tunay
Namana ko sa iyo ang kabutihang iyong taglay.

Salamat po aking mama
Nawa'y mabigyan kita ng buhay na maginhawa
Pangarap mo sa aming magkakapatid
Sana ay matupad at wala ng balakid.
Kaming magkakapatid ay nagpapasalamat ng
walang patid.

Salamat po aking mama
Ngayon ay iyong kaarawan ika-animnapo na
Pero imbes na ako ang magregalo muli ay ikaw pa
Sana sa munting tulang ito aking maipadama
Ang pagmamahal ko po at pasasalamat
Kahit sa muling buhay, ikaw pa din ang pipiliing
maging nanay. Maligayang kaarawan mahal kong
mama!

LALA...ANG ASO NI YANA

Pinapakilala ko sa inyo si Lala, alagang aso ni Yana
Sa Belgium sila nakatira
Sila ngayon ay magkahiwalay ng bahay, minsan na
lang magkita Gayunpaman, sinusulit nila bawat
oras nilang magkasama.

Si Lala ay inaalagaan ni lolo at lola
Matakaw sa manok, parang asong gala
Isang asong mapalad dahil mahal siyang talaga
Pinapaliguan at katabing matulog sa malambot na
kama.

Siya ang dakilang bantay sa bahay
Kung silang lahat ay papasok sa trabaho,
matiyagang nag-aantay Kapag may taong pa
rating, tataholan kahit kapitbahay
Siya ay maaasahang tunay.

Si Lala ay regalo kay Yana
Para may alagaan at may kalaro siya
Marunong makinig at nakakaintinding talaga
Masunuring aso, mabait na alaga

Isang araw siya ay nagkasakit
Ayaw kumain, matamlay , umiiyak ng may impit
Dinala sa doktor at agad tinurukan sa may puwit
Kinabukasan, magaling na siya at naglalaro na ulit
Salamat, kami ay laging nag-alala kay Lalang
makulit.

Mahal naming alaga
Lala ang pangalan niya
Inaantay na niya ako para makasama
Pag-uwi ko, dadalhan ko siya ng pasalubong
Paboritong manok, tiyak sa tuwa, siya'y gugulong-
gulong.

ANG PINSAN KONG MARINO

May pinsan akong marino, akin siyang ilalarawan
STEPHEN JOHN ang kaniyang pangalan,
Pero bakit parang ako ay nahihirapan
Makahana-p ng mga salitang kaniyang
kinababagayan.
Sisimulan ko na lamang ng walang hulaan
At galing lahat sa puso ko aking ituturan.

Ang mga "seaman" daw ay babaero
Na ah, tiyak aalma siya nito
Dahil pinsan ko siya, aba!, ipagtatangol ko
Kahit ang nobya niya ay ayaw paniwalaan ito
Pero huwag ng magtaka siya talaga ay maginoo.
Pinalaking mabait at pasensosyo
Mapagbigay at talaga namang matulungin na tao
Ipinagmamalaki namin, siya'y
mapagpakumbabang totoo.

Sa karagatan siya ay nakikipagsapalaran,
Hindi alintana ang pagod, puyat at kalungkutan,
Para lamang maiangat ang pamumuhay ng mga
magulang,
Maituturing na isang bagong bayani sa ating
lipunan.
Saludo ako sa tatag at tibay ng puso niya't kaisipan.

Nawa'y makakamit niya din ang kaniyang mga
mithiin,
Huwag mawawalan ng pag-asa at tunay na
panalangin,
Tanging sandata niya'y nangingibang bayaan-nais
niyang marating,
Isang araw kami ay magkikita-kita din,
At yayakap sa isa't-isa sa araw na pinakahihintay
namin.
Ang tagumpay niya ay tagumpay ng pamilya
Bagay na labis kong ikakasaya.

ANG KAIBIGAN KONG RAKITERA

Ang bansag namin sa kanya, "babaeng rakitera",
Dahil talaga namang masipag at matiyaga siya
Kulang na lang maging isa siyang biretera,
Lahat ng paligsahan malamang sasalihan niya.

Lahat ng kailangan mo, sabihin mo lang,
Agad sasagot, "pm sent" at mayroon siya niyan,
Mapaarkitekto, enhinyero, tubero pati kusinero,
Lahat ng hanap, huwag lang ng bolero.

"Kuracha" ang babaeng walang pahinga,
Ay hindi pala, Maricel ang pangalan niya,
Legpit ang tawag namin sa kaniya,
Sa sobrang kasinupan sa buhay, apilyedo niya,
sinasabuhay pa.

Sa biyayang umaapaw puso niya ay palaging
humihiyaw,

Sa pagmamahal mga anak na siyang dahilan ng
kaniyang paghataw, Masusuklian din nila lahat ng
sakripisyo niya balang araw,
Dahil yan ang regalo ng Diyos sa kanyang laging
nakatanaw.

Huwag sanang mawalan ng pagasa, itong
rakiterang maganda,
Upang sa mga raket niya, buhay ay sasagana,
Andito naman kami palaging nakasuporta,
Mahal namin siya ng bonggang-bongga.

ANG PINSAN KONG TALENTADO

Tayo ay nilikha ng ating Amang makapangyarihan,
Na may kaniya-kaniyang katangian,
Lahat ay pantay-pantay sa kaniyang kaharian,
Pero ang pinsan ko'y pinuno ng talento at
kakayahan,
Para magamit niya ito sa kabutihan ng kanyang
kapwa at sa lahat ng mamamayan.

Unahin natin ang talento niya sa pag-awit, kahit
noong nasa Dubai siya ay talaga namang kaniyang
bitbit,
Hindi man siya bumibirit pero ang mga awitin
niya'y galing lahat sa puso at damdaming
walang hinanakit.
Puro kasayahan ang nais niyang ipabatid sa
kaniyang mga taga pakinig.

Magaling din siya sa pagguhit, pagsasadula,
pananahi at pagluluto. Aktibo siya sa paaralan

noon at lahat yata ng paligsahan ay kaniya ng
sinalihan, at uuwing may napanalunan.
Magaling din sya sa sayawan, palagi siyang
tinatawag sa tuwing may programa kahit pa ito ay
sa kabilang bayan.
Abah!, sikat ata siya, syempre pinsan ko yan!.

Pagdating sa kakayahan nangunguna din yan,
Diskarte sa buhay, uy!, madami siya niyan,
Lahat ng trabaho ay kaniyang nasubukan at
pinasukan para lamang makamit mga pangarap na
inaasam,
Huwag kang mag-alala at makakamit mo din lahat
yan sa tinakdang oras para sa iyo ng ating
Panginoong makapangyarihan.

Itinuring ko na bilang isa sa aking mga kapatid,
sapagkat siya ay inalagaan din ng lolo at lola kong
iniibig.
Madami man siyang pinagdaanan sa buhay,
malungkot man o masaya, lahat yan kaniyang
pinagtagumpayan.
Marami ka pang paglalakbay na gagawin aking
pinsan, DEXTER ang pangalan,
Pero alam kong saan ka man mapadpad pagdating
ng araw,
Mauuna kaming pamilya mo sa kagalakan dahil sa
wakas narating mo ang tagumpay na iyong
pinapangarap.
Mahal ka namin at ipagpatuloy mo ang iyong
paglalakbay bitbit ang kabutihan ng puso at
kagandahang asal na taglay.

TAMIS NG UNANG PAG-IBIG

Ako ay napapangiti, halos mamula-mula ang
pisngi,
Kung maalala ko ang tamis ng iyong mga sinabi,
Nuong hinahatid mo pa ako bago maggabi,
At sinusundo para sabay mananghali.

Ako'y masaya at talaga namang tuwang-tuwa,
Kapag kasama ka halos oras ay hindi alintana,
Ganyan ata talaga ang pagibig na dala,
Ng taong nagmamahal at umiibig ng dakila.

Panahong tayo ay mga bata pa,
Halos sungkitin ang buwan pati mga tala

Ngayong tayo ay tumatanda na,
Isa na lang itong matalinghagang kabanata.

Para sa aking unang pag-ibig,
Mananatili kang nasa pusong pumipintig,
May lugar kang nakalaan, kahit isa ka nang
nakaraan,
Akin itong pinagpapasalamat kasama ng
kasaysayan.
Paalam na hindi panghangganan!

ARAW NG PAGKILALA

Ang araw na ito ay napaka espesyal
Dahil sa araw na ito ay makikilala ka ng personal
Makikita at makakamayan, sa isang kodakan
Ikaw na uliran na aking hinahangaan

Eksaytcd akong makikilala ka, pangulo ng ating
embahada
Ang Embahada ng Pilipinas, Consul General RALY
L. TEJADA
Kagalang-galang at talaga namang hinahangaan.

Narito po kaming taga Horizons, para magbigay
ng simpleng mensahe, Salamat po pinuno, kayo po
ay pinagmamalaki
Hindi niyo pinababayaan ang kapakanan ng ating
mga kababayan,
Lalo na sa ganitong panahon, napakarami ang
nangangailangan.

Mabuhay po kayo at patnubayan palagi ng Poong
Maykapal,
Yan po ang aming dalanging para sa inyo ay
gumabay,
I ngatan po ang inyong sarili at kalusugan,
Para madami pa kayong kababaan na matulungan,
Mabuhay po kayo at salamat sa serbisyong totoo
Isa pong karangalan ang makasama po kayo sa
araw na ito.

KASAL O SAKAL

Isang sagradong seremonya
Idinaraos para maging ganap na mag-asawa
Kasal nga ba ang tawag dito
O sakal na sa makabagong mundo?

Ang kasal ay pag-iisang dibdib
Nang dalawang taong puno ng pag-ibig
Ang sakal naman ay pag-iisang lubid
Nang dalawang taong magkaiba ang ibig.

Bawat panig may reklamo
Makalipas lamang ang ilang bagyo
Bakit agad ang mga pagbabago
Ganito nga ba ang dapat kahinatnan nito?

Huwag sanang hayaang mawala
Ang pagmamahal sa bawat isa
Alalahanin palagi ang sagradong biyaya

Na tinanggap sa harap ng Diyos at ng buong
madla.

Kasal man yan o sakal
Ang mahalaga tayo ay magtagal
Sa relasyong may mabuting basbas
Ilawan sana ng Poong Maykapal ang ating landas
Sa bubuuin nating tahanan
Dalangin nati'y ang habambuhay na kalakasan.

Pagsasama natin ay asahang may gulo
Dahil ang pagsubok ay kaakibat natin dito sa
mundo
Mahalagang makinig sa bawat siphayo
Pagpapatawad sa isa't isa para sa payapang puso
Ang paraiso natin ay mabubuo
Dahil sa kagustuhan natin at hindi nang ibang tao.

Malayo pa ang ating lalakbayin
Sana tayo ay lalong pagtibayin
Nang ating pabaong dalangin
'Yan lamang ang kaya at lubos na hangarin
Humayo tayo at magparami, 'yan ang isa pang
tagubilin.

ABOUT THE AUTHOR

Annaliza Villegas Aquino is my name. My childhood friends call me Liezle but most of my Hongkong friends call me Anna. I was born at Laoac, Pangasinan Philippines, and a mother of 2 responsible adult kids aged 21 and 19 respectively. My nursery days were spent at Holy Rosary Academy and continued my primary days at CASCALINTA Elementary School until 1993. I decided to study at the University of the East, Manila to finish my secondary years until 1997. I studied Bachelor of Science in Civil Engineering at MAPUA Institute of Technology but unfortunately just reached my 4th year degree until the year 2000.

I worked in Hongkong for 9 years from September 7, 2011 until December 15, 2020.

I am a person who has big dreams and I never stop reaching them. One of my weaknesses is lack of self-confidence and I am shy when talking publicly. So I'm expressing my aspirations through words, writing is my way to express my emotions and I'm glad that I can inspire others through my poems. I am a fighter and full of optimism, giving all my best in everything i do.

I became a part of One Step Closer#4: Family is Everything and performed my piece "Family" on October 18, 2020 and performed also in the Carnival of Poetry: Poets of Hong Kong on November 22, 2020 and read my two poems entitled "My Purpose in Life" and "No Man is an Island" inspiring those who are weary and feeling lonely. Life is short. Always be happy.